Story of the Eye

Georges Bataille
STORY OF THE EYE
by Lord Auch

Translated by Joachim Neugroschel

CITY LIGHTS BOOKS
San Francisco

Originally published in France in 1928 as Histoire de l'oeil

© 1967 by Jean Jacques Pauvert, Paris
© This translation Urizen Books, 1977
First City Lights Edition 1987

Cover photograph and design by Gent Sturgeon and Rex Ray

Library of Congress Cataloging-in-Publication Data

Bataille, Georges, 1897-1962.
    Story of the eye.

        Translation of: Histoire de l'oeil.
        I. Title.

PQ2603.A695H4813 1987 843'.912 87-9242
ISBN: 0-87286-209-7
ISBN 13: 978-0-87286-209-8

Visit our website: www.citylights.com

CITY LIGHTS BOOKS are edited by Lawrence Ferlinghetti and
Nancy J. Peters and published at the City Lights Bookstore,
261 Columbus Avenue, San Francisco, CA 94133.

 *Contents*

Translator's Note

Story of the Eye was George Bataille's first novel, and there were four editions, the first in 1928. The other three, known as the "new version," came out in 1940, 1941, and 1967. The "new version" differs so thoroughly in all details from the first edition that one can justifiably speak of two distinct books. Indeed, the Gallimard publication of the complete works includes both versions in its opening volume.

This American translation is based on the

original version, but the "Outline for a Sequel" comes from the fourth edition.

Of all the editions, only the final, posthumous one bore the author's name. The other three were credited to Lord Auch, a pseudonym explained in Bataille's short prose piece *Le Petit* (1943). (This section from *Le Petit* is included at the end of this volume.)

J.N.

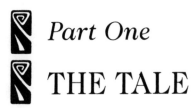

Part One

THE TALE

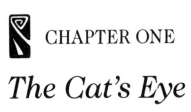

CHAPTER ONE

The Cat's Eye

I grew up very much alone, and as far back as I recall I was frightened of anything sexual. I was nearly sixteen when I met Simone, a girl my own age, at the beach in X. Our families being distantly related, we quickly grew intimate. Three days after our first meeting, Simone and I were alone in her villa. She was wearing a black pinafore with a starched white collar. I began realizing that she shared my anxiety at seeing her, and I felt even more anxious that day because I hoped she would be stark naked under the pinafore.

3

She had black silk stockings on covering her knees, but I was unable to see as far up as the cunt (this name, which I always used with Simone, is, I think, by far the loveliest of the names for the vagina). It merely struck me that by slightly lifting the pinafore from behind, I might see her private parts unveiled.

Now in the corner of a hallway there was a saucer of milk for the cat. "Milk is for the pussy, isn't it?" said Simone. "Do you dare me to sit in the saucer?"

"I dare you," I answered, almost breathless.

The day was extremely hot. Simone put the saucer on a small bench, planted herself before me, and, with her eyes fixed on me, she sat down without my being able to see her burning buttocks under the skirt, dipping into the cool milk. The blood shot to my head, and I stood before her awhile, immobile and trembling, as she eyed my stiff cock bulging in my pants. Then I lay down at her feet without her stirring, and for the first time, I saw her "pink and dark" flesh cooling in the white milk. We remained motionless, on and on, both of us equally overwhelmed . . . .

Suddenly, she got up, and I saw the milk dripping down her thighs to the stockings. She wiped herself evenly with a handkerchief as she stood over my head with one foot on the small bench, and I vigorously rubbed my cock through the pants while writhing amorously on the floor. We reached orgasm at almost the same instant without even touching one another. But when her mother came home, I was sitting in a low armchair, and I took advantage of the moment when the girl tenderly snuggled in her mother's arms: I lifted the back of her pinafore, unseen, and thrust my hand under her cunt between her two burning legs.

I dashed home, eager to jerk off some more, and the next day there were such dark rings around my eyes that Simone, after peering at me for a while, buried her head in my shoulder and said earnestly: "I don't want you to jerk off anymore without me."

Thus a love life started between the girl and myself, and it was so intimate and so driven that we could hardly let a week go by without meeting. And yet we virtually never talked about it. I realized that her feelings at seeing me were the same as mine at seeing her, but I found it difficult to have things out. I remember that one day, when we were in a car tooling along at top speed, we crashed into a cyclist, an apparently very young and very pretty girl. Her head was almost totally ripped off by the wheels. For a long time, we were parked a few yards beyond without getting out, fully absorbed in the sight of the corpse. The horror and despair at so much bloody flesh, nauseating in part, and in part very beautiful, was fairly equivalent to our usual impression upon seeing one another. Simone was tall and lovely. She was usually very natural; there was nothing heartbreaking in her eyes or her voice. But on a sensual level, she so bluntly craved any upheaval that the faintest call from the senses gave her a look directly suggestive of all things linked to deep sexuality, such as blood, suffocation, sudden terror, crime; things indefinitely destroying human bliss and honesty. I first saw her mute and absolute spasm (which I shared) the day she sat down in the saucer of milk. True, we only exchanged fixed stares at analogous moments. But we never calmed down or played except in the brief relaxed minutes after an orgasm.

I ought to say, nevertheless, that we waited a long time before copulating. We merely took any opportunity to indulge in unusual acts. We did not lack modesty—on the contrary—but something urgently drove us to defy modesty together as immodestly as possible. Thus, no sooner had she asked me never to jerk off again by myself (we had met on top of a cliff), than she pulled down my pants and had me stretch out on the ground. She tucked her dress up, mounted my belly with her back towards my face, and let herself go, while I thrust my finger, lubricated with my young jizm, into her cunt. Next, she lay down with her head under my cock between my legs, and thrusting her cunt in the air, she brought her body down towards me, while I raised my head to the level of that cunt: her knees found support on my shoulders.

"Can't you pee up to my cunt?" she said.

"Yes," I answered, "but with you like this, it'll get on your dress and your face."

"So what," she concluded. And I did as she said, but no sooner was I done than I flooded her again, this time with fine white come.

Meanwhile, the smell of the sea mixed with the smell of wet linen, our naked bodies, and the come. Evening was gathering, and we stayed in that extraordinary position, tranquil and motionless, when all at once we heard steps crumpling the grass.

"Please don't move, please," Simone begged.

The steps halted, but it was impossible to see who was approaching. Our breathing had stopped together. Simone's ass, raised aloft, did strike me as an all-powerful entreaty, perfect as it was, with its two narrow, delicate buttocks and its deep crevice; and I never doubted for an instant that the unknown man or woman would soon give in and feel compelled to jerk off endlessly while watching that ass. Now the steps resumed, faster this time, almost running, and suddenly a ravishing blond girl loomed into view: Marcelle, the purest and most poignant of our friends. But we were too strongly contracted in our dreadful positions to move even a hair's breadth, and it was our unhappy friend who suddenly collapsed and huddled in the grass amid sobs. Only now did we tear loose from our extravagant embrace to hurl ourselves upon a self-abandoned body. Simone hiked up the skirt, ripped off the panties, and drunkenly showed me a new cunt, as lovely and pure as her own: I kissed it furiously while jerking off Simone, whose legs closed around the hips of that strange Marcelle, who no longer hid anything but her sobs.

"Marcelle," I exclaimed, "please, please don't cry. I want you to kiss me on the mouth . . . ."

Simone, for her part, stroked the girl's lovely smooth hair, covering her body with fond kisses.

Meanwhile the sky had turned quite thundery, and with nightfall, huge raindrops began plopping down, bringing relief from the harshness of a torrid, airless day. The sea was loudly raging, outroared by long rumbles of thunder, while flashes of lightning, bright as day, kept brusquely revealing the two pleasured cunts of the now silent girls. A brutal frenzy drove our three bodies. Two young mouths fought over my ass, my balls, and my cock, but I still kept pushing apart female legs wet with saliva and come, splaying them as if writhing out of a monster's grip, and yet that monster was nothing but the utter violence of my movements. The hot rain was finally pouring down and streaming over our fully exposed bodies. Huge booms of thunder shook us, heightening our fury, wresting forth our cries of rage, which each flash accompanied with a glimpse of our sexual parts. Simone had found a mud puddle, and was smearing herself wildly: she was jerking off with the earth and coming violently, whipped by the downpour, my head locked in her soil-covered legs, her face wallowing in the puddle, where she was brutally churning Marcelle's cunt, one arm around Marcelle's hips, the hand yanking the thigh, forcing it open.

CHAPTER TWO

The Antique Wardrobe

That was the period when Simone developed a mania for breaking eggs with her ass. She would do a headstand on an armchair in the parlor, her back against the chair's back, her legs bent towards me, while I jerked off in order to come in her face. I would put the egg right on the hole in her ass, and she would skillfully amuse herself by shaking it in the deep crack of her buttocks. The moment my jizm shot out and trickled down her eyes, her buttocks would squeeze together and she would come while I smeared my face abundantly in her ass.

Very soon, of course, her mother, who might enter the villa parlor at any moment, did catch us in our unusual act. But still, the first time this fine woman stumbled upon us, she was content, despite having led an exemplary life, to gape wordlessly, so that we did not notice a thing. I suppose she was too flabbergasted to speak. But when we were done and trying to clean up the mess, we noticed her standing in the doorway.

"Pretend there's no one there," Simone told me, and she went on wiping her ass.

And indeed, we blithely strolled out as though the woman had been reduced to a family portrait.

A few days later, however, when Simone was doing gymnastics with me in the rafters of a garage, she pissed on her mother, who had the misfortune to stop underneath without seeing her. The sad widow got out of the way and gaped at us with such dismal eyes and such a desperate expression that she egged us on, that is to say, simply with Simone bursting into laughter, crouching on all fours on the beams and exposing her cunt to my face, I uncovered that cunt completely and jerked off while looking at it.

More than a week had passed without our seeing Marcelle, when we ran into her on the street one day. The blonde girl, timid and naively pious, blushed so deeply at seeing us, that Simone embraced her with uncommon tenderness.

"Please forgive me, Marcelle," she murmured. "What happened the other day was absurd, but that doesn't mean we can't be friends now. I promise we'll never lay a hand on you again."

Marcelle, who had an unusual lack of willpower, agreed to join us for tea with some friends at our place. But instead of tea, we drank quantities of chilled champagne.

The sight of Marcelle blushing had completely overwhelmed us. We understood one another, Simone and I, and we were certain that from now on nothing would make us shrink from achieving our ends. Besides Marcelle, there were three other pretty girls and two boys here. The oldest of the eight being not quite seventeen, the beverage soon took effect; but aside from Simone and myself, they were not as excited as we wanted them to be. A phonograph rescued us from our predicament. Simone, dancing a frenzied Charleston by herself, showed everyone her legs up to her cunt, and when the other girls were asked to dance a solo in the same way, they were in too good a mood to require coaxing. They did have panties on, but the panties bound the cunt laxly without hiding much. Only Marcelle, intoxicated and silent, refused to dance.

Finally, Simone, pretending to be dead drunk, crumbled a tablecloth and, lifting it up, she offered to make a bet.

"I bet," she said, "that I can pee into the tablecloth in front of everyone."

It was basically a ridiculous party of mostly turbulent and boastful youngsters. One of the boys challenged her, and it was agreed that the winner would fix the penalty . . . . Naturally, Simone did not waver for an instant, she richly soaked the tablecloth. But this stunning act visibly rattled her to the quick, so that all the young fools started gasping.

"Since the winner decides the penalty," said Simone to the loser, "I am now going to pull down your pants in front of everyone."

Which happened without a hitch. When his pants were off, his shirt was likewise removed (to keep him from looking ridiculous). All the same, nothing serious had occurred yet: Simone had scarcely run a light hand over her young friend, who was dazzled, drunk, and naked, yet all she could think of was Marcelle, who for several moments now had been begging me to let her leave.

"We promised we wouldn't touch you, Marcelle. Why do you want to leave?"

"Just because," she replied stubbornly, a violent rage gradually coming over her.

All at once, to everyone's horror, Simone fell upon the floor. A convulsion shook her harder and harder, her clothes were in disarray, her ass stuck in the air, as though she were having an epileptic fit. But rolling about at the foot of the boy she

had undressed, she mumbled almost inarticulately:
"Piss on me . . . Piss on my cunt . . ." she
repeated, with a kind of thirst.

Marcelle gaped at this spectacle: she blushed
again, her face was blood-red. But then she said to
me, without even seeing me, that she wanted to
take off her dress. I half tore it off, and hard upon it,
her underwear. All she had left was her stockings
and belt, and after I fingered her cunt a bit and
kissed her on the mouth, she glided across the
room to a large antique bridal wardrobe, where she
shut herself in after whispering a few words to
Simone.

She wanted to jerk off in the wardrobe and
was pleading to be left in peace.

I ought to say that we were all very drunk
and completely bowled over by what had been
going on. The naked boy was being sucked by a
girl. Simone, standing with her dress tucked up,
was rubbing her bare cunt against the wardrobe, in
which a girl was audibly jerking off with brutal
gasps. All at once, something incredible happened,
a strange swish of water, followed by a trickle and a
stream from under the wardrobe door: poor Marcelle was pissing in her wardrobe while jerking off.
But the explosion of totally drunken guffaws that
ensued rapidly degenerated into a debauche of
tumbling bodies, lofty legs and asses, wet skirts and
come. Guffaws emerged like foolish and involun-

tary hiccups but scarcely managed to interrupt a brutal onslaught on cunts and cocks. And yet soon we could hear Marcelle dismally sobbing alone, louder and louder, in the makeshift pissoir that was now her prison.

Half an hour later, when I was less drunk, it dawned on me that I ought to let Marcelle out of her wardrobe: the unhappy girl, naked now, was in a dreadful state. She was trembling and shivering feverishly. Upon seeing me, she displayed a sickly but violent terror. After all, I was pale, smeared with blood, my clothes askew. Behind me, in unspeakable disorder, ill bodies, brazenly stripped, were sprawled about. During the orgy, shards of glass had left deep bleeding cuts in two of us. A young girl was throwing up, and all of us had exploded in such wild fits of laughter at some point or other that we had wet our clothes, an armchair, or the floor. The resulting stench of blood, sperm, urine, and vomit made me almost recoil in horror, but the inhuman shriek from Marcelle's throat was far more terrifying. I must say, however, that Simone was sleeping tranquilly by now, her belly up, her hand still on her beaver, her pacified face almost smiling.

Marcelle, staggering wildly across the room with shrieks and snarls, looked at me again. She flinched back as though I were a hideous ghost in a nightmare, and she collapsed in a jeremiad of howls that grew more and more inhuman.

Astonishingly, this litany brought me to my senses. People were running up, it was inevitable. But I never for an instant dreamt of fleeing or lessening the scandal. On the contrary, I resolutely strode to the door and flung it open. What a spectacle, what joy! One can readily picture the cries of dismay, the desperate shrieks, the exaggerated threats of the parents entering the room! Criminal court, prison, the guillotine were evoked with fiery yells and spasmodic curses. Our friends themselves began howling and sobbing in a delirium of tearful screams; they sounded as if they had been set afire as live torches. Simone exulted with me!

And yet, what an atrocity! It seemed as if nothing could terminate the tragicomical frenzy of these lunatics, for Marcelle, still naked, kept gesticulating, and her agonizing shrieks of pain expressed unbearable terror and moral suffering; we watched her bite her mother's face amid arms vainly trying to subdue her.

Indeed, by bursting in, the parents managed to wipe out the last shreds of reason, and in the end, the police had to be called, with all the neighbors witnessing the outrageous scandal.

 CHAPTER THREE

Marcelle's Smell

My own parents had not turned up that evening with the pack. Nevertheless, I judged it prudent to decamp and elude the wrath of an awful father, the epitome of a senile Catholic general. I entered our villa by the back door and filched a certain amount of money. Next, quite convinced they would look for me everywhere but there, I took a bath in my father's bedroom. Finally, by around ten o'clock, I was out in the open country, having left the following note on my mother's night table: "I beseech you not to send the police after me for I am carrying a gun, and the first bullet will be for the policeman, the second for myself."

I have never had any aptitude for what is known as striking a pose, and in this circumstance in particular, I only wished to keep my family at bay, for they relentlessly hated scandal. Still, having written the note with the greatest levity and not without laughing, I thought it might not be such a bad idea to pocket my father's revolver.

I walked along the seashore most of the night, but without getting very far from X because of all the windings of the coast. I was merely trying to soothe a violent agitation, a strange, spectral delirium in which, willy-nilly, phantasms of Simone and Marcelle took shape with gruesome expressions. Little by little, I even thought I might kill myself, and, taking the revolver in hand, I managed to lose any sense of words like hope or despair. But in my weariness, I realized that my life *had* to have some meaning all the same, and *would* have one if only certain events, defined as desirable, were to occur. I finally accepted being so extraordinarily haunted by the names *Simone* and *Marcelle*. Since it was no use laughing, I could keep going only by accepting or feigning to imagine a phantastic compromise that would confusedly link my most disconcerting moves to theirs.

I slept in a wood during the day, and at nightfall I went to Simone's place: I passed through

the garden by climbing over the wall. My friend's
bedroom was lit, and so I cast some pebbles
through the window. A few seconds later she came
down and almost wordlessly we headed towards
the beach. We were delighted to see one another
again. It was dark out, and from time to time I
lifted her dress and took hold of her cunt, but it
didn't make me come—quite the opposite. She sat
down and I stretched out at her feet. I soon felt that
I could not keep back my sobs, and I really cried
for a long time on the sand.

"What's wrong?" asked Simone.

And she gave me a playful kick. Her foot
struck the gun in my pocket and a fearful bang
made us shriek at the same time. I wasn't wounded
but I was up on my feet as though in a different
world. Simone stood before me, frighteningly pale.

That evening we didn't even think of jerking
each other off, but we remained in an endless
embrace, mouth to mouth, something we had
never done before.

This is how I lived for several days: Simone
and I would come home late at night and sleep in
her room, where I would stay locked in until the
following night. Simone would bring me food. Her
mother, having no authority over her (the day of
the scandal, she had gone for a walk the instant she
heard the shrieks), accepted the situation without
even trying to fathom the mystery. As for the ser-
vants, money had for some time been ensuring

their devotion to Simone.

In fact, it was they who told us of the circumstances of Marcelle's confinement and even the name of the sanitarium. From the very first day, all we worried about was Marcelle: her madness, the loneliness of her body, the possibilities of getting to her, helping her to escape, perhaps. One day, when I tried to rape Simone in her bed, she brusquely slipped away:

"You're totally insane, little man," she cried, "I'm not interested—here, in a bed like this, like a housewife and mother! I'll only do it with Marcelle!"

"What are you talking about?" I asked, disappointed, but basically agreeing with her.

She came back affectionately and said in a gentle, dreamy voice:

"Listen, she won't be able to help pissing when she sees us . . . making it."

I felt a hot, enchanting liquid run down my legs, and when she was done, I got up and in turn watered her body, which she complaisantly turned to the unchaste and faintly murmuring spurt on her skin. After thus flooding her cunt, I smeared jizm all over her face. Full of muck, she climaxed in a liberating frenzy. She deeply inhaled our pungent and happy odor: "You smell like Marcelle," she buoyantly confided after a hefty climax, her nose under my wet ass.

Obviously Simone and I were sometimes

taken with a violent desire to fuck. But we no longer thought it could be done without Marcelle, whose piercing cries kept grating our ears, for they were linked to our most violent desires. Thus it was that our sexual dream kept changing into a nightmare. Marcelle's smile, her freshness, her sobs, the sense of shame that made her redden and, painfully red, tear off her own clothes and surrender lovely blond buttocks to impure hands, impure mouths, beyond all the tragic delirium that had made her lock herself in the wardrobe to jerk off with such abandon that she could not help pissing—all these things warped our desires, so that they endlessly racked us. Simone, whose conduct during the scandal had been more obscene than ever (sprawled out, she had not even covered herself, in fact she had flung her legs apart)— Simone could not forget that the unforeseen orgasm provoked by her own brazenness, by Marcelle's howls and the nakedness of her writhing limbs, had been more powerful than anything she had ever managed to picture before. And her cunt would not open to me unless Marcelle's ghost, raging, reddening, frenzied, came to make her brazenness overwhelming and far-reaching, as if the sacrilege were to render everything generally dreadful and infamous.

At any rate, the swampy regions of the cunt (nothing resembles them more than the days of flood and storm or even the suffocating gaseous eruptions of volcanoes, and they never turn active except, like storms or volcanoes, with something of catastrophe or disaster)—those hearbreaking regions, like Simone, in an abandon presaging only violence, allowed me to stare hypnotically, were nothing for me now but the profound, subterranean empire of a Marcelle who was tormented in prison and at the mercy of nightmares. There was only one thing I understood: how utterly the orgasms ravaged the girl's face with sobs interrupted by horrible shrieks.

And Simone, for her part, no longer viewed the hot, acrid come that she caused to spurt from my cock without seeing it muck up Marcelle's mouth and cunt.

"You could smack her face with your come," she confided to me, while smearing her cunt—"till it sizzles," as she put it.

CHAPTER FOUR

A Sunspot

Other girls and boys no longer interested us. All we could think of was Marcelle, and already we childishly imagined her hanging herself, the secret burial, the funeral apparitions. Finally, one evening, after getting the precise information, we took our bicycles and pedaled off to the sanitarium where our friend was confined. In less than an hour, we had ridden the twenty kilometers separating us from a sort of castle within a walled park on an isolated cliff overlooking the sea. We had learned that Marcelle was in Room 8, but obviously we would have to get inside the building to find her. Now all we could hope for was to climb in her window after sawing through the bars, and we were at a loss how to identify her window among thirty others, when our attention was drawn to a strange apparition. We had scaled the wall and were now in the park, among trees buffeted by a violent gust, when we spied a second-story window opening and a shadow holding a sheet and fastening it to one of the bars. The sheet promptly smacked in the gusts, and the window was shut before we could recognize the shadow.

It is hard to imagine the harrowing racket of that vast white sheet caught in the squall. It greatly outroared the fury of the sea or the wind in the trees. That was the first time I saw Simone racked by anything but her own lewdness: she huddled against me with a beating heart and gaped at the huge phantom raging in the night as though dementia itself had hoisted its colors on this lugubrious château.

We were motionless, Simone cowering in my arms and I half-haggard, when all at once the wind seemed to tatter the clouds, and the moon, with a revealing clarity, poured sudden light on something so bizarre and so excruciating for us that an abrupt, violent sob choked up in Simone's throat: at the center of the sheet flapping and banging in the wind, a broad wet stain glowed in the translucent moonlight . . .

A few seconds later, new black clouds plunged everything into darkness again, but I stayed on my feet, suffocating, feeling my hair in the wind, and weeping wretchedly, like Simone herself, who had collapsed in the grass, and for the first time, her body was quaking with huge, child-like sobs.

It was our unfortunate friend, no doubt about it, it was Marcelle who had opened that light-less window, Marcelle who had tied that stunning signal of distress to the bars of her prison. She had obviously jerked off in bed with such a disorder of her senses that she had entirely inundated herself, and it was then that we saw her hang the sheet from the window to let it dry.

As for myself, I was at a loss about what to do in such a park, with that bogus *château de plaisance* and its repulsively barred windows. I walked around the building, leaving Simone upset and sprawling on the grass. I had no practical goal, I just wanted to take a breath of air by myself. But then, on the side of the château, I stumbled upon an unbarred open window on the ground floor; I felt for the gun in my pocket and I entered cautiously: it was a very ordinary parlor. An electric flashlight helped me to reach an antechamber; then a stairway. I could not distinguish anything, I did not get anywhere, the rooms were not numbered. Besides, I was incapable of understanding anything, as though I were hexed: at that moment,

I could not even understand why I had the idea of removing my pants and continuing that anguishing exploration only in my shirt. And yet I stripped off my clothes, piece by piece, leaving them on a chair, keeping only my shoes on. With a flashlight in my left hand and the revolver in my right hand, I wandered aimlessly, haphazardly. A rustle made me switch off my lamp quickly. I stood motionless, whiling away the time by listening to my erratic breath. Long, anxious minutes wore by without my hearing any more noise, and so I flashed my light back on, but a faint cry sent me fleeing so swiftly that I forgot my clothes on the chair.

I sensed I was being followed: so I hurriedly climbed out through the window and hid in a garden lane: but no sooner had I turned to observe what might be happening in the château than I spied a naked woman in the window frame; she jumped into the park as I had done and ran off towards a thorn bush.

Nothing was more bizarre for me in those utterly thrilling moments than my nudity against the wind on the path of that unknown garden. It was as if I had left the earth, especially because the squall was as violent as ever, but warm enough to suggest a brutal entreaty. I did not know what to do with the gun which I still held in my hand, for I had no pockets left; by charging after the woman who had run past me unrecognized, I would obviously be hunting her down to kill her. The roar of the wrathful elements, the raging of the trees and the sheet, also helped to prevent me from discerning anything distinct in my will or in my gestures.

All at once, I halted, out of breath: I had reached the bushes where the shadow had disappeared. Inflamed by my revolver, I began looking about, when suddenly it seemed as if all reality were tearing apart: a hand, moistened by saliva, had grabbed my cock and was jerking it, a slobbering, burning kiss was planted on the root of my ass, the naked chest and legs of a woman pressed against my legs with an orgasmic jolt. I scarcely had time to spin around when come burst in the face of my wonderful Simone: clutching my revolver, I was swept up by a thrill as violent as the storm, my teeth chattered and my lips foamed, with twisted arms I gripped my gun convulsively, and, willy-nilly, three blind, horrifying shots were fired in the direction of the château.

Drunk and limp, Simone and I had fled from one another and raced across the park like dogs; the squall was far too wild now for the gunshots to awake any of the sleeping tenants in the château, even if the bangs were heard on the inside. But when we instinctively looked up at Marcelle's window above the sheet slamming the wind, we were greatly surprised to see that one of the bullets had left a star-shaped crack in one of the panes. The window shook, opened, and the shadow appeared a second time.

Dumbstruck, as though about to see Marcelle bleed and fall dead in the windowframe, we remained standing under the strange, nearly motionless apparition. Because of the furious wind, we were incapable of even making ourselves heard.

"What did you do with your clothes?" I asked Simone an instant later. She said she had been looking for me and, unable to track me down, she had finally gone to search the interior of the château; but before clambering through the window, she had undressed, figuring she "would feel more free." And when she had come back out after me, terrified by me, she found that the wind had carried off her dress. Meanwhile, she kept observing Marcelle, and it never crossed her mind to ask me why *I* was naked.

The girl in the window disappeared. A moment that seemed immense crawled by: she switched on the light in her room. Finally, she came back to breathe the open air and gaze at the ocean. Her sleek, pallid hair was caught in the wind, we could make out her features: she had not changed, but now there was something wild in her eyes, something restless, contrasting with the still childlike simplicity of her features. She looked thirteen rather than sixteen. Under her nightgown, we could distinguish her thin but full body, firm, unobtrusive, and as beautiful as her fixed stare.

When she finally caught sight of us, the surprise seemed to restore life to her face. She called, but we couldn't hear. We beckoned. She blushed up to her ears. Simone, weeping almost, while I lovingly caressed her forehead, sent her kisses, to which she responded without smiling. Next, Simone ran her hand down her belly to her beaver. Marcelle imitated her, and poising one foot on the sill, she exposed a leg sheathed in a white silk stocking almost up to her blond cunt. Curiously, she was wearing a white belt and white stockings, whereas black-haired Simone, whose cunt was in my hand, was wearing a black belt and black stockings.

Meanwhile, the two girls were jerking off with terse, brusque gestures, face to face in the howling night. They were nearly motionless, and tense, and their eyes gaped with unrestrained joy. But soon, some invisible monstrosity appeared to be yanking Marcelle away from the bars, though her left hand clutched them with all her might. We saw her tumble back into her delirium. And all that remained before us was an empty, glowing window, a rectangular hole piercing the opaque night, showing our aching eyes a world composed of lightning and dawn.

CHAPTER FIVE

A Trickle of Blood

Urine is deeply associated for me with salt-peter; and lightning, I don't know why, with an antique chamber pot of unglazed earthenware, lying abandoned one rainy autumn day on the zinc roof of a provincial wash house. Since that first night at the sanitarium, those wrenching images were closely knit, in the obscurest part of my brain, with the cunt and the drawn and dismal expression I had sometimes caught on Marcelle's face. But then, this chaotic and dreadful landscape of my imagination was suddenly inundated by a stream of light and blood, for Marcelle could climax only by drenching herself, not with blood, but with a spurt of urine that was limpid and even illuminated for me, at first violent and jerky like hiccups, then free and relaxed and coinciding with an outburst of superhuman happiness. It is not astonishing that the bleakest and most leprous aspects of a dream are merely an urging in that direction, an obstinate waiting for total joy, like the vision of that glowing hole, the empty window, for example, at the very moment when Marcelle lay sprawling on the floor, endlessly inundating it.

But that day, in the rainless tempest, Simone and I, our clothing lost, were forced to leave the château, fleeing like animals through the hostile darkness, our imaginations haunted by the despondency that was bound to take hold of Marcelle again, making the wretched inmate almost an embodiment of the fury and terror that kept driving our bodies to endless debauchery. We soon found our bicycles and could offer one another the irritating and theoretically unclean sight of a naked though shod body on a machine. We pedalled rapidly, without laughing or speaking, peculiarly satisfied with our mutual presences, akin to one another in the common isolation of lewdness, weariness, and absurdity.

Yet we were both literally perishing of fatigue. In the middle of a slope, Simone halted, saying she had the shivers. Our faces, backs, and legs were bathed in sweat, and we vainly ran our hands over one another, over the various parts of our soaked and burning bodies; despite a more and more vigorous massage, she was all trembling flesh and clattering teeth. I stripped off one of her stockings to wipe her body, which gave out a hot odor recalling the beds of sickness or debauchery. Little by little, however, she came around to a more bearable state, and finally she offered me her lips as a token of gratitude.

I was still extremely agitated. We had ten more kilometers to go, and in the state we were in, we obviously had to reach X by dawn. I could barely keep upright and despaired of ever reaching the end of this ride through the impossible. We had abandoned the real world, the one made up solely of dressed people, and the time elapsing since then was already so remote as to seem almost beyond reach. Our personal hallucination now developed as boundlessly as perhaps the total nightmare of human society, for instance, with earth, sky, and atmosphere.

A leather seat clung to Simone's bare cunt, which was inevitably jerked by the legs pumping up and down on the spinning pedals. Furthermore, the rear wheel vanished indefinitely to my eyes, not only in the bicycle fork but virtually in the crevice of the cyclist's naked ass: the rapid whirling of the dusty tire was also directly comparable to both the thirst in my throat and my erection, which ultimately had to plunge into the depths of the cunt sticking to the bicycle seat. The wind had died down somewhat, and part of the starry sky was visible. And it struck me that death was the sole outcome of my erection, and if Simone and I were killed, then the universe of our unbearable personal vision was certain to be replaced by the pure stars, fully unrelated to any external gazes and realizing in a cold state, without human delays or detours, something that strikes me as the goal of my sexual licentiousness: a geometric incandescence (among other things, the coinciding point of life and death, being and nothingness), perfectly fulgurating.

Yet, these images were, of course, tied to the contradiction of a prolonged state of exhaustion and an absurd rigidity of my penis. Now it was difficult for Simone to see this rigidity, partly because of the darkness, and partly because of the swift rising of my left leg, which kept hiding my stiffness by turning the pedal. Yet I felt I could see her eyes, aglow in the darkness, peer back constantly, no matter how fatigued, at this breaking point of my body, and I realized she was jerking off more and more vehemently on the seat, which was pincered between her buttocks. Like myself, she had not yet drained the tempest evoked by the shamelessness of her cunt, and at times she let out husky moans; she was literally torn away by joy, and her nude body was hurled upon an embankment with an awful scraping of steel on the pebbles and a piercing shriek.

I found her inert, he head hanging down, a thin trickle of blood running from the corner of her mouth. Horrified to the limit of my strength, I pulled up one arm, but it fell back inert. I threw myself upon the lifeless body, trembling with fear, and as I clutched it in an embrace, I was overcome with bloody spasms, my lower lip drooling and my teeth bared like a leering moron.

Meanwhile, Simone was slowly coming to: her arm touched me in an involuntary movement, and I quickly returned from the torpor overwhelming me after I had besmirched what I thought was a corpse. No injury, no bruise marked the body, which was still clad in the garter belt and a single stocking. I took her in my arms and carried her down the road, heedless of my fatigue; I walked as fast as I could because the day was just breaking, but only a superhuman effort allowed me to reach the villa and happily put my marvelous friend alive in her very own bed.

The sweat was pissing from my face and all over my body, my eyes were bloody and swollen, my ears screeching, my teeth chattering, my temples and my heart drumming away. But since I had just rescued the person I loved most in the world, and since I thought we would soon be seeing Marcelle, I lay down next to Simone's body just as I was, soaked and full of coagulated dust, and soon I drifted off into vague nightmares.

CHAPTER SIX

Simone

One of the most peaceful eras of my life was the period following Simone's minor accident, which only left her ill. Whenever her mother came, I would step into the bathroom. Usually, I took advantage of these moments to piss or even bathe; the first time the woman tried to enter, she was immediately stopped by her daughter:

"Don't go in," she said, "there's a naked man in there."

Each time, however, the mother was dismissed before long, and I would take my place again in a chair next to the sickbed. I smoked cigarettes, went through newspapers, and if there were any items about crime or violence, I would read them aloud. From time to time, I would carry a feverish Simone to the bathroom to help her pee, and then I would carefully wash her on the bidet. She was extremely weak and naturally I never stroked her seriously; but nevertheless, she soon delighted in having me throw eggs into the toilet bowl, hard-boiled eggs, which sank, and shells sucked out in various degrees to obtain varying levels of immersion. She would sit for a long time, gazing at the eggs. Then she would settle on the toilet to view them under her cunt between the parted thighs; and finally, she would have me flush the bowl.

Another game was to crack a fresh egg on the edge of the bidet and empty it under her: sometimes she would piss on it, sometimes she had me strip naked and swallow the raw egg from the bottom of the bidet. She did promise that as soon as she was well again, she would do the same for me and also for Marcelle.

At that time, we imagined Marcelle, with her dress tucked up, but her body covered and her feet shod: we would put her in a bath tub filled with fresh eggs, and she would pee while crushing them. Simone also daydreamed about my holding Marcelle, this time with nothing on but her garter-belt and stockings, her cunt aloft, her legs bent, and her head down; Simone herself, in a bathrobe drenched in hot water and thus clinging to her body but exposing her bosom, would then get up on a white enameled chair with a cork seat. I would arouse her breasts from a distance by lifting the tips on the heated barrel of a long service revolver that had been loaded and just fired (first of all, this would shake us up, and secondly, it would give the barrel a pungent smell of powder). At the same time, she would pour a jar of dazzling white *crème fraîche* on Marcelle's gray anus, and she would also urinate freely in her robe or, if the robe were ajar, on Marcelle's back or head, while I could piss on Marcelle from the other side (I would certainly piss on her breasts). Furthermore, Marcelle herself could fully inundate me if she liked, for while I held her up, her thighs would be gripping my neck. And she could also stick my cock in her mouth, and what not.

It was after such dreams that Simone would ask me to bed her down on blankets by the toilet, and she would rest her head on the rim of the bowl and fix her *wide eyes* on the *white eggs*. I myself settled comfortably next to her so that our cheeks and temples might touch. We were calmed by the long contemplation. The gulping gurgle of the flushing water always amused Simone, making her forget her obsession and ultimately restoring her high spirits.

At last, one day at six, when the oblique

sunshine was directly lighting the bathroom, a half-sucked egg was suddenly invaded by the water, and after filling up with a bizarre noise, it was ship-wrecked before our very eyes. This incident was so extraordinarily meaningful to Simone that her body tautened and she had a long climax, virtually drinking my left eye between her lips. Then, with-out leaving the eye, which was sucked as obsti-nately as a breast, she sat down, wrenching my head toward her on the seat, and she pissed noisily on the bobbing eggs with total vigor and satisfaction.

As of now she could be regarded as cured, and she demonstrated her joy by speaking to me at length about various intimate things, whereas ordinarily she never spoke about herself or me. Smiling, she admitted that an instant ago, she had felt a strong urge to relieve herself completely, but had held back for the sake of greater pleasure. Truly, the urge bloated her belly and particularly made her cunt swell up like a ripe fruit; and when I passed my hand under the sheets and her cunt gripped it firm and tight, she remarked that she was still in the same state and that it was inordinately pleasant. Upon my asking what the word *urinate* reminded her of, she replied: *terminate*, the eyes, with a razor, something red, the sun. And *egg?* A calf's eye, because of the color of the head (the calf's head) and also because the white of the egg was the white of the eye, and the yolk the eyeball. The eye, she said, was egg-shaped. She asked me to promise that when we could go outdoors, I would fling eggs into the sunny air and break them with shots from my gun, and when I replied that it was out of the question, she talked on and on, trying to reason me into it. She played gaily with words, speaking about *broken eggs*, and then *broken eyes*, and her arguments became more and more unreasonable.

She added that, for her, the smell of the ass was the smell of powder, a jet of urine a "gunshot seen as a light;" each of her buttocks was a peeled hard-boiled egg. We agreed to send for hot soft-boiled eggs without shells, for the toilet, and she promised that when she now sat on the seat, she would ease herself fully on those eggs. Her cunt was still in my hand and in the state she had described; and after her promise, a storm began brewing little by little in my innermost depth—I was reflecting more and more.

It is fair to say that the room of a bedridden invalid is just the right place for gradually rediscovering childhood lewdness. I gently sucked Simone's breast while waiting for the soft-boiled eggs, and she ran her fingers through my hair. Her mother was the one who brought us the eggs, but I didn't even turn around, I assumed it was a maid, and I kept on sucking the breast contentedly. Nor was I ultimately disturbed when I recognized the voice, but since she remained and I couldn't pass up even one instant of my pleasure, I thought of pulling down my pants as for a call of nature, not ostentatiously, but merely hoping she would leave and delighted at going beyond all limits. When she finally decided to walk out and vainly ponder over her dismay elsewhere, the night was already gathering, and we switched on the lamp in the bathroom. Simone settled on the toilet, and we each ate one of the hot eggs with salt. With the three that were left, I softly caressed her body, gliding them between her buttocks and thighs, then I slowly dropped them into the water one by one. Finally, after viewing them for a while, immersed, white, and still hot (this was the first time she was seeing them peeled, that is naked, drowned under her beautiful cunt), Simone continued the immersion with a plopping noise akin to that of the soft-boiled eggs.

But I ought to say that nothing of the sort ever happened between us again, and, *with one exception,* no further eggs ever came up in our conversations; nevertheless, if we chanced to notice one or more, we could not help reddening when our eyes met in a silent and murky interrogation.

At any rate, it will be shown by the end of this tale, that this interrogation was not to remain without an answer indefinitely, and above all, that this unexpected answer is necessary for measuring the immensity of the void that yawned before us, without our knowledge, during our singular entertainments with the eggs.

CHAPTER SEVEN

Marcelle

By a sort of shared modesty, Simone and I had always avoided talking about the most important objects of our obsessions. That was why the word *egg* was dropped from our vocabulary, and we never spoke about the kind of interest we had in one another, even less about what Marcelle meant to us. We spent all of Simone's illness in a bedroom, looking forward to when we could go back to Marcelle, as nervously as we had once waited for the end of the last class in school, and so all we talked about was the day we would return to the château. I had prepared a small cord, a thick, knotted rope, and a hacksaw, all of which Simone examined with the keenest interest, peering attentively at each knot and section of the rope. I also managed to find the bicycles, which I had concealed in a thicket the day of our tumble, and I meticulously oiled the various parts, the gears, ball bearings, sprockets, etc. I then attached a pair of toe-clips to my own bicycle so that I could seat one of the girls in back. Nothing could be easier, at least for the time being, than to have Marcelle living in Simone's room secretly like myself. We would simply be forced to share the bed (and we would inevitably have to use the same bathtub, etc.).

But a good six weeks passed before Simone could pedal after me reasonably well to the sanitarium. Like the previous time, we left at night: in fact, I still kept out of sight during the day, and this time there was certainly every reason for remaining inconspicuous. I was in a hurry to arrive at the place that I dimly regarded as a "haunted castle," due to the association of the words *sanitarium* and *castle,* and also the memory of the phantom sheet and the thought of the lunatics in a huge silent dwelling at night. But now, to my surprise, even though I was ill at ease anywhere in the world, I felt at bottom as if I were going home. And that was indeed my impression when we jumped over the park wall and saw the huge building stretching out ahead beyond the trees: only Marcelle's window was still aglow and wide open. Taking some pebbles from a lane, we threw them into her chamber and they promptly summoned the girl, who quickly recognized us and obeyed our gesture of putting a finger on our lips. But of course we also held up the knotted rope to let her understand what we were doing this time. I hurled the cord up to her with the aid of a rock, and she threw it back after looping it around a bar. There were no difficulties, the big rope was hoisted by Marcelle and fastened to the bar, and I scrambled all the way up.

Marcelle flinched when I tried to kiss her. She merely watched me very attentively as I started filing away at a bar. Since she only had a bathrobe on, I softly told her to get dressed so she could come with us. She simply turned her back to pull flesh-colored stockings over her legs, securing them on a belt of bright red ribbons that brought out an ass with a perfect shape and an exceptionally fine skin. I continued filing, bathed in sweat because of both my effort and what I saw. Her back still towards me, Marcelle pulled a blouse over long, flat hips, whose straight lines were admirably terminated by the ass when she had one foot on a chair. She did not slip on any panties, only a pleated, gray woolen skirt and a sweater with very tiny black, white, and red checks. After stepping into flat-heeled shoes, she came over to the window and sat down close enough to me so that my one hand could caress her head, her lovely short hair, so sleek and so blond that it actually looked pale. She gazed at me affectionately and seemed touched by my wordless joy at seeing her.

"Now we can get married, can't we?" she finally said, gradually won over. "It's very bad here, we suffer . . . ."

At that point, I would never have dreamt for even an instant that I could do anything but devote the rest of my life to such an unreal apparition. She let me give her a long kiss on her forehead and her eyes, and when one of her hands happened to touch my leg, she looked at me wide-eyed, but before withdrawing her hand, she ran it over my clothes absent-mindedly.

After long work, I succeeded in cutting through the filthy bar. I pulled it aside with all my strength, which left enough space for her to squeeze through. She did so, and I helped her descend, climbing down underneath, which forced me to see the top of her thigh and even to touch it when I supported her. Reaching the ground, she snuggled in my arms and kissed my mouth with all her strength, while Simone, sitting at our feet, her eyes wet with tears, flung her hands around Marcelle's legs, hugging her knees and thighs. At first, she only rubbed her cheek against the thigh, but then, unable to restrain a huge surge of joy, she finally yanked the body apart, pressing her lips to the cunt, which she greedily devoured.

However, Simone and I realized that Marcelle grasped absolutely nothing of what was going on and she was actually incapable of telling one situation from another. Thus she smiled, imagining how aghast the director of the "haunted castle" would be to see her strolling through the garden with her husband. Also, she was scarcely aware of Simone's existence; mirthfully, she at times mistook her for a wolf because of her black hair, her silence, and because Simone's head was docilely rubbing Marcelle's thigh, like a dog nuzzling his master's leg. Nonetheless, when I spoke to Marcelle about the "haunted castle," she did not ask me to explain; she understood that this was the building where she had been wickedly locked up. And whenever she thought of it, her terror pulled her away from me as though she had seen something pass through the trees. I watched her uneasily, and since my face was already hard and somber, I too frightened her, and almost at the same instant she asked me to protect her *when the Cardinal returned.*

We were lying in the moonlight by the edge of a forest. We wanted to rest a while during our trip back and we especially wanted to embrace and stare at Marcelle.

"But who is the Cardinal?" Simone asked her.

"The man who locked me in the wardrobe," said Marcelle.

"But why is he a cardinal?" I cried.

She replied: "Because he is the priest of the guillotine."

I now recalled Marcelle's dreadful fear when she left the wardrobe, and particularly two details: I had been wearing a blinding red carnival novelty, a Jacobine liberty cap; furthermore, because of the deep cuts in a girl I had raped, my face, clothes, hands—all parts of me were stained with blood.

Thus, in her terror, Marcelle confused a cardinal, a priest of the guillotine, with the blood-smeared executioner wearing a liberty cap: a bizarre overlapping of piety and abomination for priests explained the confusion, which, for me, has remained attached to both my hard reality and the horror continually aroused by the compulsiveness of my actions.

CHAPTER EIGHT

The Open Eyes of the Deadwoman

For a moment, I was totally helpless after this unexpected discovery; and so was Simone. Marcelle was now half asleep in my arms, so that we didn't know what to do. Her dress was pulled up, exposing the gray beaver between red ribbons at the end of long thighs, and it had thereby become an extraordinary hallucination in a world so frail that a mere breath might have changed us into light. We didn't dare budge, and all we desired was for that unreal immobility to last as long as possible, and for Marcelle to fall sound asleep.

My mind reeled in some kind of exhausting

vertigo, and I don't know what the outcome would have been if Simone, whose worried gaze ricocheted between my eyes and Marcelle's nudity, had not made a sudden, gentle movement: she opened her thighs, saying in a blank voice that she couldn't hold back any longer.

She soaked her dress in a long convulsion that fully denuded her and promptly made me spurt a wave of jizm in my clothes.

I stretched out in the grass, my skull on a large, flat rock and my eyes staring straight up at the milky way, that strange breach of astral sperm and heavenly urine across the cranial vault formed by the ring of constellations: that open crack at the summit of the sky, apparently made of ammoniacal vapors shining in the immensity (in empty space, where they burst forth absurdly like a rooster's crow in total silence), a broken egg, a broken eye, or my own dazzled skull weighing down the rock, bouncing symmetrical images back to infinity. The nauseating crow of a rooster in particular coincided with my own life, that is to say, now, the Cardinal, because of the crack, the red color, the discordant shrieks he provoked in the wardrobe, and also because one cuts the throats of roosters.

To others, the universe seems decent because decent people have gelded eyes. That is why they fear lewdness. They are never frightened by the crowing of a rooster or when strolling under a starry heaven. In general, people savor the "pleasures of the flesh" only on condition that they be insipid.

But as of then, no doubt existed for me: I did not care for what is known as "pleasures of the flesh" because they really are insipid; I cared only for what is classified as "dirty." On the other hand, I was not even satisfied with the usual debauchery, because the only thing it dirties is debauchery itself, while, in some way or other, anything sublime and perfectly pure is left intact by it. My kind of debauchery soils not only my body and my thoughts, but also anything I may conceive in its course, that is to say, the vast starry universe, which merely serves as a backdrop.

I associate the moon with the vaginal blood of mothers, sisters, that is, the menstrua with their sickening stench . . . .

I loved Marcelle without mourning her. If she died, then it was my fault. If I had nightmares, if I sometimes locked myself up in a cellar for hours at a time precisely because I was thinking about Marcelle, I would nevertheless still be prepared to start all over again, for instance by dunking her hair, head down, in a toilet bowl. But since she is dead, I have nothing left but certain catastrophes that bring me to her at times when I least expect it. Otherwise, I cannot possibly perceive the least kinship now between the dead girl and myself, which makes most of my days inevitably dreary.

I will merely report here that Marcelle hanged herself after a dreadful incident. She recognized the huge bridal wardrobe, and her teeth started chattering: she instantly realized upon looking at me that *I* was the man she called the Cardinal, and when she began shrieking, there was no other way for me to stop that desperate howling than to leave the room. By the time Simone and I returned she was hanging inside the wardrobe . . . .
I cut the rope, but she was quite dead. We laid her out on the carpet. Simone saw I was getting a hard-on and she started jerking me off. I too stretched out on the carpet. It was impossible to otherwise; Simone was still a virgin, and I fucked her for the first time, next to the corpse. It was very painful for both of us, but we were glad precisely because it *was* painful. Simone stood up and gazed at the corpse. Marcelle had become a total stranger, and in fact, so had Simone at that moment. I no longer cared at all for either Simone or Marcelle. Even if someone had told me it was I who had just died, I would not even have been astonished, so alien were these events to me. I observed Simone, and, as I precisely recall, my only pleasure was in the smutty things Simone was doing, for the corpse was very irritating to her, as though she could not bear the thought that this

creature, so similar to her, could not feel her any-more. The open eyes were more irritating than anything else. Even when Simone drenched the face, those eyes, extraordinarily, did not close. We were perfectly calm, all *three* of us, and that was the most hopeless part of it. Any boredom in the world is linked, for me, to that moment and, above all, to an obstacle as ridiculous as death. But that won't prevent me from thinking back to that time with no revulsion and even with a sense of com-plicity. Basically, the lack of excitement made everything far more absurd, and thus Marcelle was closer to me dead than in her lifetime, inasmuch as absurd existence, so I imagine, has all the prerogatives.

As for the fact that Simone dared to piss on the corpse, whether in boredom or, at worst, in irritation: it mainly goes to prove how impossible it was for us to understand what was happening, and of course, it is no more understandable today than back then. Simone, being truly incapable of con-ceiving death such as one normally considers it, was frightened and furious, but in no way awe-struck. Marcelle belonged to us so deeply in our isolation that we could not see her as just another corpse. Nothing about her death could be mea-sured by a common standard, and the contradic-tory impulses overtaking us in this circumstance neutralized one another, leaving us blind and, as it were, very remote from anything we touched, in a world where gestures have no carrying power, like voices in a space that is absolutely soundless.

CHAPTER NINE

Lewd Animals

To avoid the bother of a police investigation, we instantly took off for Spain, where Simone was counting on our disappearing with the help of a fabulously rich Englishman, who had offered to support her and would be more likely than anyone else to show interest in our plight.

The villa was abandoned in the middle of the night. We had no trouble stealing a boat, reaching an obscure point on the Spanish coast, and burning up the craft with the aid of two drums of gasoline we had taken along, as a precautionary measure, from the garage of the villa. Simone left me concealed in a wood during the day and went to look for the Englishman in San Sebastian. She only came back at nightfall, but driving a magnificent automobile, with suitcases full of linen and rich clothing.

Simone said that Sir Edmond would join us in Madrid and all day long he had been plying her with the most detailed questions about Marcelle's death, making her draw diagrams and sketches. Finally he had told a servant to buy a wax mannequin with a blonde wig; he had then laid the figure out on the floor and asked Simone to urinate on its face, on the open eyes, in the same position as she had urinated on the eyes of the corpse: during all that time, Sir Edmond had not even touched her.

However, there had been a great change in Simone after Marcelle's suicide—she kept staring into space all the time, looking as if she belonged to something other than the terrestrial world, where almost everything bored her; or if she *was* still attached to this world, then purely by way of orgasms, that were rare, but incomparably more violent than before. These orgasms were as different from normal climaxes as, say, the mirth of savage Africans from that of Occidentals. In fact, though the savages may sometimes laugh as moderately as whites, they also have long-lasting jags, with all parts of the body in violent release, and

they go whirling willy-nilly, flailing their arms
about wildly, shaking their bellies, necks, and
chests, and chortling and gulping horribly. As for
Simone, she would first open uncertain eyes, at
some lewd and dismal sight . . . .

For example, Sir Edmond had a cramped,
windowless pigsty, where one day he locked up a
petite and scrumptious streetwalker from Madrid;
wearing only cami-knickers, she collapsed in a
pool of liquid manure under the bellies of the
grunting swine. Once the door was shut, Simone
had me fuck her on and on, in front of that door,
with her ass in the mud, under a fine drizzle of rain,
while Sir Edmond jerked off.

Gasping and slipping away from me, Simone
grabbed her own ass in both hands and threw back
her head, which banged violently against the
ground; she tensed breathlessly for a few seconds,
pulling with all her might on the fingernails buried
in her ass, then tore herself away at one swoop and
thrashed about on the ground like a headless
chicken, hurting herself with a terrible bang on the
door fittings. Sir Edmond gave her his wrist to bite
on and allay the spasm that kept shaking her, and I
saw that her face was smeared with saliva and
blood.

After these huge fits, she always came to
nestle in my arms; she settled her little ass comfortably in my large hands and remained there for a

long time without moving or speaking, huddled like a little girl, but always somber.

Sir Edmond deployed his ingenuity at providing us with obscene spectacles at random, but Simone still preferred bullfights. There were actually three things about bullfights that fascinated her: the first, when the bull comes hurtling out of the bullpen like a big rat; the second, when its horns plunge all the way into the flank of a mare; the third, when that ludicrous, raw-boned mare gallops across the arena, lashing out unseasonably and dragging a huge, vile bundle of bowels between her thighs in the most dreadful wan colors, a pearly white, pink, and gray. Simone's heart throbbed fastest when the exploding bladder dropped its mass of mare's urine on the sand in one quick plop.

She was on tenterhooks from start to finish at the bullfight, in terror (which of course mainly expressed a violent desire) at the thought of seeing the toreador hurled up by one of the monstrous lunges of the horns when the bull made its endless, blindly raging dashes at the void of colored cloths. And there is something else I ought to say: When the bull makes its quick, brutal, thrusts over and over again into the matador's cape, barely grazing the erect line of the body, any spectator has that feeling of total and repeated lunging typical of the game of coitus. The utter nearness of death is also felt in the same way. But these series of prodigious passes are rare. Thus, each time they occur, they unlease a veritable delirium in the arena, and it is well known that at such thrilling instants the women jerk off by merely rubbing their thighs together.

Apropos bullfights, Sir Edmond once told Simone that until quite recently, certain virile Spaniards, mostly occasional amateur toreadors, used to ask the caretaker of the arena to bring them the fresh, roasted balls of one of the first bulls to be killed. They received them at their own seats, in the front row of the arena, and ate them while watching the killing of the next few bulls. Simone took a keen interest in this tale, and since we were attending the first major bullfight of the year that Sunday, she begged Sir Edmond to get her the balls of the first bull, but added one condition: they had to be raw.

"I say," objected Sir Edmond, "whatever do you want with raw balls? You certainly don't intend to eat raw balls now, do you?"

"I want to have them before me on a plate," concluded Simone.

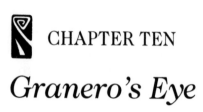

CHAPTER TEN

Granero's Eye

On May 7, 1922, the toreadors La Rosa, Lalanda, and Granero were to fight in the arena of Madrid; the last two were renowned as the best matadors in Spain, and Granero was generally considered superior to Lalanda. He had only just turned twenty, yet he was already extremely popular, being handsome, tall and of a still childlike simplicity. Simone had been deeply interested in his story, and, exceptionally, had shown genuine pleasure when Sir Edmond announced that the celebrated bull-killer had agreed to dine with us the evening of the fight.

Granero stood out from the rest of the matadors because there was nothing of the butcher about him; he looked more like a very manly prince charming with a perfectly elegant figure. In this respect, the matador's costume is quite expressive, for it safeguards the straight line shooting up so rigid and erect every time the lunging bull grazes the body and because the pants so tightly sheathe the ass. A bright red cloth and a brilliant sword (before the dying bull whose hide steams with sweat and blood) complete the metamorphosis, bringing out the most captivating feature of the game. One must also bear in mind the typically torrid Spanish sky, which never has the color or harshness one imagines: it is just perfectly sunny with a dazzling but mellow sheen, hot, turbid, at times even unreal when the combined intensities of light and heat suggest the freedom of the senses.

Now this extreme unreality of the solar blaze was so closely attached to everything happening to me during the bullfight on May 7, that the only objects I have ever carefully preserved are a round paper fan, half yellow, half blue, that Simone had that day, and a small illustrated brochure with a description of all the circumstances and a few photographs. Later on, during an embarkment, the small valise containing those two souvenirs tumbled into the sea, and was fished out by an Arab with a long pole, which is why the objects are in such a bad state. But I need them to fix that event to the earthly soil, to a geographic point and a precise date, an event that my imagination compulsively pictures as a simple vision of solar deliquescence.

The first bull, the one whose raw balls Simone looked forward to having served on a plate, was a kind of black monster, who zoomed out of the pen so quickly that despite all efforts and all shouts, he disemboweled three horses in a row before an orderly fight could take place; one horse and rider were hurled aloft together, loudly crashing down behind the horns. But when Granero faced the bull, the combat was launched with brio, proceeding amid a frenzy of cheers. The young man sent the furious beast racing around him in his pink cape; each time, his body was lifted by a sort of spiraling jet, and he just barely eluded a frightful impact. In the end, the death of the solar monster was performed cleanly, with the beast blinded by a scrap of red cloth, the sword deep in the blood-smeared body. An incredible ovation resounded as the bull staggered to its knees with the uncertainty of a drunkard, collapsed with its legs sticking up, and died.

Simone, who sat between Sir Edmond and myself, witnessed the killing with an exhileration at least equal to mine, and she refused to sit down again when the interminable acclamation for the young man was over. She took my hand wordlessly and led me to an outer courtyard of the filthy arena, where the stench of equine and human urine was suffocating because of the great heat. I grabbed Simone's cunt, and she seized my furious cock through my pants. We stepped into a stinking shithouse, where sordid flies whirled about in a sunbeam. Standing here, I exposed Simone's cunt, and into her blood-red, slobbery flesh I stuck my fingers, then my penis, which entered that cavern of blood while I jerked off her ass, thrusting my bony middle finger deep inside. At the same time, the revolts of our mouths cleaved together in a storm of saliva.

A bull's orgasm is not more powerful than the one that wrenched through our loins to tear us to shreds, though without shaking my thick penis out of that stuffed vulva, which was gorged with come.

Our hearts were still booming in our chests, which were equally burning and equally lusting to press stark naked against wet unslaked hands, and Simone's cunt was still as greedy as before and my cock stubbornly rigid, as we returned to the first row of the arena. But when we arrived at our places next to Sir Edmond, there, in broad sunlight, on Simone's seat, lay a white dish containing two peeled balls, glands the size and shape of eggs, and of a pearly whiteness, faintly bloodshot, like the globe of an eye: they had just been removed from the first bull, a black-haired creature, into whose body Granero had plunged his sword.

"Here are the raw balls," Sir Edmond said to Simone in a light British accent.

Simone was already kneeling before the plate, peering at it in absorbed interest, but also in an unwonted quandary. Apparently, she wanted to do something but didn't know how to go about it, which exasperated her. I picked up the dish to let her sit down, but she grabbed it away from me with a categorical "no" and returned it to the stone seat.

Sir Edmond and I were growing annoyed at being the focus of our neighbors' attention just when the bullfight was slackening. I leaned over and whispered to Simone, asking what had gotten into her.

"Idiot!" she replied. "Can't you see I want to sit on the plate, and all these people watching!"

"That's absolutely out of the question," I rejoined, "sit down."

At the same time, I took away the dish and made her sit, and I stared at her to let her know that I understood, that I remembered the dish of milk, and that this renewed desire was unsettling me. From that moment on, neither of us could keep from fidgeting, and this state of malaise was contagious enough to affect Sir Edmond. I ought to

say that the fight had become boring, unpugna-
cious bulls were facing matadors who didn't know
what to do next; and to top it off, since Simone had
demanded seats in the sun, we were trapped in
something like an immense vapor of light and
muggy heat, which parched our throats as it bore
down upon us.

It really was totally out of the question for
Simone to lift her dress and place her bare behind
in the dish of raw balls. All she could do was hold
the dish in her lap. I told her I would like to fuck
her again before Granero returned to fight the
fourth bull, but she refused, and she sat there,
keenly involved, despite everything, in the disem-
bowlments of horses, followed, as she childishly put
it, by "loss and noise," namely the cataract of
bowels.

Little by little, the sun's radiance sucked us
into an unreality that fitted our malaise—the
wordless and powerless desire to explode and kick
up our asses. We grimaced, because our eyes were
blinded and because we were thirsty, our senses
ruffled, and there was no possibility of quenching
our desires. We three had managed to share in the
morose dissolution that leaves no harmony between
the various spasms of the body. We were so far
gone that even Granero's return could not pull us
out of that stupefying absorption. Besides, the bull
opposite him was distrustful and seemed unre-
sponsive; the combat went on just as drearily as
before.

The events that followed were without transition or connection, not because they weren't actually related, but because my attention was so absent as to remain absolutely dissociated. In just a few seconds: first, Simone bit into one of the raw balls, to my dismay; then Granero advanced towards the bull, waving his scarlet cloth; finally, almost at once, Simone, with a blood-red face and a suffocating lewdness, uncovered her long white thighs up to her moist vulva, into which she slowly and surely fitted the second pale globule— Granero was thrown back by the bull and wedged against the balustrade; the horns struck the balustrade three times at full speed; at the third blow, one horn plunged into the right eye and through the head. A shriek of unmeasured horror coincided with a brief orgasm for Simone, who was lifted up from the stone seat only to be flung back with a bleeding nose, under a blinding sun; men instantly rushed over to haul away Granero's body, the right eye dangling from the head.

 CHAPTER ELEVEN

Under the Sun of Seville

Thus, two globes of equal size and consistency had suddenly been propelled in opposite directions at once. One, the white ball of the bull, had been thrust into the "pink and dark" cunt that Simone had bared in the crowd; the other, a human eye, had spurted from Granero's head with the same force as a bundle of innards from a belly. This coincidence, tied to death and to a sort of urinary liquefaction of the sky, first brought us back to Marcelle in a moment that was so brief and almost insubstantial, yet so uneasily vivid that I stepped forward like a sleepwalker as though about to touch *her* at eye level.

Needless to say, everything was promptly back to normal, though with blinding obsessions in the hour after Granero's death. Simone was in such a foul mood that she told Sir Edmond she wouldn't spend another day in Madrid; she was very anxious to see Seville because of its reputation as a city of pleasure.

Sir Edmond took a heady delight in satisfying the whims of "the simplest and most angelic creature ever to walk the earth," and so the next day he accompanied us to Seville, where we found an even more liquefying heat and light than in Madrid. A lavish abundance of flowers in the streets, geraniums and rose laurels, helped to put our senses on edge.

Simone walked about naked under a white dress that was flimsy enough to hint at the red garter-belt underneath, and, in certain positions, even at her beaver. Furthermore, everything in this city contributed to making her radiate such sensuality that when we passed through the torrid streets, I often saw the cocks stand up in trousers.

Indeed, we virtually never stopped having sex. We avoided orgasms and we went sight-seeing, for this was the only way to keep from having my penis endlessly immersed in her fur. But we did take advantage of any opportunities when we were out. We would leave one convenient place with never any goal but to find another like it. An empty museum room, a stairway, a garden path lined with high bushes, an open church, deserted alleys in the evenings—we walked until we found the right place, and the instant we found it, I would open the girls' body by lifting one of her legs and shoving my cock to the bottom of her cunt in one swoop. A few moments later, I would pull my steaming member from its stable, and our promenade would continue almost aimlessly. Usually, Sir Edmond would follow at a distance in order to surprise us: he would turn purple, but he never came over. And if he jerked off, he would do it discreetly, not for caution's sake, of course, but because he never did anything unless standing isolated and almost utterly steady, with a dreadful muscular contraction.

"This is a very interesting place," he said one day in regard to a church, "it's the church of Don Juan."

"So what?" replied Simone.

"Stay here with me," Sir Edmond said to me. "And you, Simone, you ought to go round this church all by yourself."

"What an awful idea!"

Nevertheless, however awful the idea, it aroused her curiosity, and she went in by herself while we waited in the street.

Five minutes later, Simone reappeared at the threshold of the church. We were dumbstruck: not only was she guffawing her head off, but she couldn't speak or stop laughing, so that, partly by contagion, partly because of the intense light, I began laughing as hard as she, and so did Sir Edmond to a certain extent.

"Bloody girl," he said. "Can't you explain? By the bye, we're laughing right over the tomb of Don Juan!"

And laughing even harder, he pointed at a large church brass at our feet. It was the tomb of the church's founder, who, the guides claimed, was Don Juan: after repenting, he had himself buried under the doorstep so that the faithful would trudge over his corpse when entering or leaving their haunt.

·But now our wild laughter burst out again tenfold. In our mirth, Simone had lightly pissed down her legs, and a tiny trickle of water had landed on the brass.

We noted a further effect of her accident: the thin dress, being wet, stuck to her body, and since the cloth was now fully transparent, Simone's attractive belly and thighs were revealed with particular lewdness, a dark patch between the red ribbons of her garter belt.

"All I can do is go into the church," said Simone, a bit calmer, "it'll dry."

We burst into a large space, where Sir Edmond and I vainly looked for the comical sight that the girl had been unable to explain. The room was relatively cool, and the light came from win-

dows, filtering through curtains of a bright red,
transparent cretonne. The ceiling was of carved
woodwork, the walls were plastered but encum-
bered with religious gewgaws more or less gilded.
The entire back wall was covered from floor to rafters by an altar and a giant Baroque retable of
gilded wood; the involved and contorted decorations conjured up India, with deep shadows and
golden glows, and the whole altar at first seemed
very mysterious and just right for sex. At either side
of the entrance door hung two famous canvases by
the painter Valdès Leal, pictures of decomposing
corpses: interestingly, one of the eye sockets was
being gnawed through by a rat. Yet in all these
things, there was nothing funny to be found.

Quite the contrary: the whole place was
sumptuous and sensuous, the play of shadows and
light from the red curtains, the coolness and a
strong pungent aroma of blossoming oleander,
plus the dress sticking to Simone's beaver—
everything was urging me to burst loose and bare
that wet cunt on the floor, when I spied a pair of
silk shoes at a confessional: the feet of a penitent
female.

"I want to see them leave," said Simone.

She sat down before me, not far from the
confessional, and all I could do was caress her
neck, the line of her hair, or her shoulders with my
cock. And that put her so much on edge that she
told me to tuck my penis away immediately or she

would rub it till I shot my load.

I had to sit down and merely look at Simone's nakedness through the soaked cloth, at best in the open air, when she wanted to fan her wet thighs and she uncrossed them and lifted her dress.

"You'll see," she said.

That was why I patiently waited for the key to the puzzle. After a rather long wait, a very beautiful young brunette stepped out of the confessional, her hands folded, her face pale and enraptured: with her head thrown back and her eyes white and vacant, she slowly eased across the room like an opera ghost. There was something so truly unexpected about the whole thing that I desperately squeezed my legs together to keep from laughing, when the door of the confessional opened: someone else emerged, this time a blond priest, very young, very handsome, with a long thin face and the pale eyes of a saint. His arms were crossed on his chest, and he remained on the threshhold of the booth, gazing at a fixed point on the ceiling as though a celestial apparition were about to help him levitate.

The priest thus moved in the same direction as the woman, and he would probably have vanished in turn without seeing anything if Simone, to my great surprise, had not brought him up sharply. Something unbelievable had occurred to her: she greeted the visionary courteously and said she wanted to confess.

The priest, still gliding in his ecstasy, indicated the confessional with a distant gesture and reentered his tabernacle, softly closing the door without a word.

CHAPTER TWELVE

Simone's Confession and Sir Edmond's Mass

One can readily imagine my stupor at watching Simone kneel down by the cabinet of the lugubrious confessor. While she confessed her sins, I waited, extremely anxious to see the outcome of such an unexpected action. I assumed this sordid creature was going to burst from his booth, pounce upon the impious girl, and flagellate her. I was even getting ready to knock the dreadful phantom down and treat him to a few kicks; but nothing of the sort happened: the booth remained closed, Simone spoke on and on through the tiny grilled window, and that was all.

I was exchanging sharply interrogative looks with Sir Edmond when things began to grow clear: Simone was slowly scratching her thigh, moving her legs apart; keeping one knee on the prayer stool, she shifted one foot to the floor, and she was exposing more and more of her legs over her stockings while still murmuring her confession. At times she even seemed to be jerking off.

I softly drew up at the side to try and see what was happening: Simone really *was* jerking off, the left part of her face was pressed against the grille near the priest's head, her limbs tensed, her thighs splayed, her fingers rummaging deep in the fur; I was able to touch her, I bared her cunt for an instant. At that moment, I distinctly heard her say:

"Father, I still have not confessed the worst sin of all."

A few seconds of silence.

"The worst sin of all is very simply that I'm jerking off while talking to you."

More seconds of whispering inside, and finally almost aloud:

"If you don't believe me, I can show you."

And indeed, Simone stood up and spread one thigh before the eye of the window while jerking off with a quick, sure hand.

"Okay, priest," cried Simone, banging away at the confessional, "what are you doing in your shack there? Jerking off, too?"

But the confessional kept its peace.

"Well, then I'll open."

And Simone pulled out the door.

Inside, the visionary, standing there with a lowered head, was mopping a sweat-bathed brow. The girl groped for his cock under the cassock: he didn't turn a hair. She pulled up the filthy black skirt so that the long cock stuck out, pink and hard: all he did was throw back his head with a grimace, and a hiss escaped through his teeth, but he didn't interfere with Simone, who shoved the bestiality into her mouth and took long sucks on it.

Sir Edmond and I were immobile in our stupor. For my part, I was spellbound with admiration, and I didn't know what else to do, when the enigmatic Englishman resolutely strode to the confessional and, after edging Simone aside as delicately as could be, yanked the larva out of its hole by its wrist, and flung it brutally at our feet: the vile priest lay there like a cadaver, his teeth to the ground, not uttering a cry. We promptly carried him to the vestry.

His fly was open, his cock dangling, his face livid and drenched with sweat, he didn't resist, but breathed heavily: we put him in a large wooden armchair with architectural decorations.

"*Señores,*" the wretch sniveled, "you must think I'm a hypocrite."

"No," replied Sir Edmond with a categorical intonation.

Simone asked him: "What's your name?"

"Don Aminado," he answered.

Simone slapped the sacerdotal pig, which gave the pig another hard-on. We stripped off all his clothes, and Simone crouched down and pissed on them like a bitch. Then she jerked and sucked the pig while I urinated in his nostrils. Finally, to top off this cold exaltation, I fucked Simone in the ass while she violently sucked his cock.

Meanwhile, Sir Edmond, contemplating the scene with his characteristic hard-labour face, carefully inspected the room where we had found refuge. He glimpsed a tiny key hanging from a nail in the woodwork.

"What is that key for?" he asked Don Aminado.

From the expression of dread on the priest's face, Sir Edmond realized it was the key to the tabernacle.

The Englishman returned a few moments later, carrying a ciborium of twisted gold, decorated with a quantity of angels as naked as cupids. The wretched Don Aminado gaped at this receptacle of consecrated hosts on the floor, and his handsome moronic face, already contorted because Simone was flagellating his cock with her teeth and tongue, was now fully gasping and panting.

After barricading the door, Sir Edmond rummaged through the closets until he finally lit upon a large chalice, whereupon he asked us to abandon the wretch for an instant.

"Look," he explained to Simone, "the eucharistic hosts in the ciborium, and here the chalice where they put white wine."

"They smell like come," said Simone, sniffing the unleavened wafers.

"Precisely," continued Sir Edmond. "The hosts, as you see, are nothing other than Christ's sperm in the form of small white biscuits. And as for the wine they put in the chalice, the ecclesiastics say it is the *blood* of Christ, but they are obviously mistaken. If they really thought it was the blood, they would use *red* wine, but since they employ only *white* wine, they are showing that at the bottom of their hearts they are quite aware that this is urine."

The lucidity of this logic was so convincing that Simone and I required no further explanation. She, armed with the chalice and I with the ciborium, the two of us marched over to Don Aminado, who was still inert in his armchair, faintly agitated by a slight quiver through his body.

Simone began by slamming the base of the chalice against his skull, which jolted him and left him utterly dazed. Then she resumed sucking him, which provoked his ignoble rattles. After bringing his senses to a height of fury with Sir Edmond's help and mine, she gave him a hard shake.

"That's not all," she said in a voice that brooked no reply. "It's time to piss."

And she struck his face again with the chalice, but at the same time she stripped naked before him and I finger-fucked her.

Sir Edmond's gaze, fixed on the stunned eyes of the young cleric, was so imperious that the thing went off with barely any hitch; Don Aminado noisily poured his urine into the chalice, which Simone held under his thick cock.

"And now, drink," commanded Sir Edmond.

The paralyzed wretch drank with a well-nigh filthy ecstasy at one long gluttonous draft. Again Simone sucked and jerked him; he continued guzzling tragically and reveling in it. With a demented gesture, he bashed the sacred chamber-pot against a wall. Four robust arms lifted him up and, with open thighs, his body erect, and yelling like a pig being slaughtered, he spurted his come on the hosts in the ciborium, which Simone held in front of him while jerking him off.

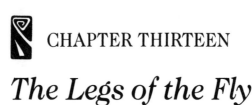

CHAPTER THIRTEEN

The Legs of the Fly

He dropped the swine and he crashed to the floor. Sir Edmond, Simone, and myself were coldly animated by the same determination, together with an incredible excitement and levity. The priest lay there with a limp cock, his teeth digging into the floor with rage and shame. Now that his balls were drained, his abomination appeared to him in all its horror. He audibly sighed:

"Oh miserable sacrileges . . . ."

And other incomprehensible laments.

Sir Edmond nudged him with his foot; the

monster leaped up and drew back, bellowing with such ludicrous fury that we burst out laughing.

"Get on your feet," Sir Edmond ordered him, "you're going to screw this girl."

"Wretches . . . " Don Aminado threatened in a choking voice, "Spanish police . . . prison . . . the garrotte . . . ."

"But you are forgetting that is your jizm," observed Sir Edmond.

A ferocious grimace, a trembling like that of a cornered beast, and then: "The garrotte for me too. But you three . . . first."

"Poor fool," smirked Sir Edmond. "*First!* Do you think I am going to let you wait that long? *First!*"

The imbecile gaped dumbstruck at the Englishman: an extremely silly expression darted across his handsome face. Something like an absurd joy began to open his mouth, he crossed his arms over his naked chest and finally gazed at us with ecstatic eyes. "Martyrdom . . . " he uttered in a voice that was suddenly feeble and yet tore out like a sob. "Martyrdom . . . ." A bizarre hope of purification had come to the wretch, illuminating his eyes.

"First I am going to tell you a story," Sir Edmond said to him sedately. "You know that men who are hanged or garrotted have such stiff cocks the instant their respiration is cut off, that they ejaculate. You are going to have the pleasure of being martyred while fucking this girl."

And when the horrified priest rose to defend himself, the Englishman brutally knocked him down, twisting his arm.

Next, Sir Edmond, slipping under his victim, pinioned his arms behind his back while I gagged him and bound his legs with a belt. The Englishman, gripping his arms from behind in a stranglehold, disabled the priest's legs in his own. Kneeling in back, I kept the man's head immobile between my thighs.

"And now," said Sir Edmond to Simone, "mount this little padre."

Simone removed her dress and squatted on the belly of this singular martyr, her cunt next to his flabby cock.

"Now," continued Sir Edmond, "squeeze his throat, the pipe just behind the Adam's apple: a strong, gradual pressure."

Simone squeezed, a dreadful shudder ran through that mute, fully immobilized body, and the cock stood on end. I took it into my hands and had no trouble fitting it into Simone's vulva, while she continued to squeeze the throat.

The utterly intoxicated girl kept wrenching the big cock in and out with her buttocks, atop a body whose muscles were cracking in our formidable strangleholds.

At last, she squeezed so resolutely that an even more violent thrill shot through her victim, and she felt the come shooting inside her cunt. Now she let go, collapsing backwards in a tempest of joy.

Simone lay on the floor, her belly up, her thigh still smeared by the dead man's sperm which had trickled from her vulva. I stretched out at her side to rape and fuck her in turn, but all I could do was squeeze her in my arms and kiss her mouth, because of a strange inward paralysis ultimately caused by my love for the girl and the death of the unspeakable creature. I have never been so content.

I didn't even stop Simone from pushing me aside and going to view her work. She straddled the naked cadaver again, scrutinizing the purplish face with the keenest interest, she even sponged the sweat off the forehead and obstinately waved away a fly buzzing in a sunbeam and endlessly flitting back to alight on the face. All at once, Simone uttered a soft cry. Something bizarre and quite baffling had happened: this time, the insect had perched on the corpse's eye and was agitating its long nightmarish legs on the strange orb. The girl took her head in her hands and shook it, trembling, then she seemed to plunge into an abyss of reflections.

Curiously, we weren't the least bit worried about what might happen. I suppose if anyone had come along, Sir Edmond and I wouldn't have given him much time to be scandalized. But no matter. Simone gradually emerged from her stupor and sought protection with Sir Edmond, who stood motionless, his back to the wall; we could hear the fly flitting over the corpse.

"Sir Edmond," she said, rubbing her cheek gently on his shoulder, "I want you to do something."

"I shall do anything you like," he replied.

She made me come over to the corpse: she knelt down and completely opened the eye that the fly had perched on.

"Do you see the eye?" she asked me.

"Well?"

"It's an egg," she concluded in all simplicity.

"Okay," I urged her, extremely disturbed, "what are you getting at?"

"I want to play with this eye."

"What do you mean?"

"Listen, Sir Edmond," she finally let it out, "you must give me this eye at once, tear it out at once, I want it!"

Sir Edmond was always poker-faced except when he turned purple. Nor did he bat an eyelash now; but the blood did shoot to his face. He removed a pair of fine scissors from his wallet, knelt down, then nimbly inserted the fingers of his left hand into the socket and drew out the eye, while his right hand snipped the obstinate ligaments. Next, he presented the small whitish eyeball in a hand reddened with blood.

Simone gazed at the absurdity and finally

took it in her hand, completely distraught; yet she had no qualms, and instantly amused herself by fondling the depth of her thighs and inserting this apparently fluid object. The caress of the eye over the skin is so utterly, so extraordinarily gentle, and the sensation is so bizarre that it has something of a rooster's horrible crowing.

Simone meanwhile amused herself by slipping the eye into the profound crevice of her ass, and after lying down on her back and raising her legs and ass, she tried to keep the eye there simply by squeezing her buttocks together. But all at once, it zoomed out like a pit squooshed from a cherry, and dropped on the thin belly of the corpse, an inch or so from the cock.

In the meantime, I had let Sir Edmond undress me, so that I could pounce stark naked on the crunching body of the girl; my entire cock vanished at one lunge into the hairy crevice, and I fucked her hard while Sir Edmond played with the eye, rolling it, in between the contortions of our bodies, on the skin of our bellies and breasts. For an instant, the eye was trapped between our navels.

"Put it in my ass, Sir Edmond," Simone shouted. And Sir Edmond delicately glided the eye between her buttocks.

But finally, Simone left me, grabbed the beautiful eyeball from the hands of the tall Englishman, and with a staid and regular pressure from her hands, she slid it into her slobbery flesh, in the midst of the fur. And then she promptly drew me over, clutching my neck between her arms and smashing her lips on mine so forcefully that I climaxed without touching her and my come shot all over her fur.

Now I stood up and, while Simone lay on her side, I drew her thighs apart, and found myself facing something I imagine I had been waiting for in the same way that a guillotine waits for a neck to slice. I even felt as if my eyes were bulging from my head, erectile with horror; in *Simone's* hairy vagina, I saw the wan blue eye of *Marcelle,* gazing at me through tears of urine. Streaks of come in the steaming hair helped give that dreamy vision a disastrous sadness. I held the thighs open while Simone was convulsed by the urinary spasm, and the burning urine streamed out from under the eye down to the thighs below . . . .

Two hours later, Sir Edmond and I were sporting false black beards, and Simone was bedizened in a huge, ridiculous black hat with yellow flowers and a long cloth dress like a noble girl from the provinces. In this get-up, we rented a car and left Seville. Huge valises allowed us to change our personalities at every leg of the journey in order to outwit the police investigation. Sir Edmond evinced a humorous ingenuity in these circumstances: thus we marched down the main street of the small town of Ronda, he and I dressed as Spanish priests, wearing the small hairy felt hats and priestly cloaks, and manfully puffing on big cigars; as for Simone, who was walking between us in the costume of a Seville seminarist, she looked more angelic than ever. In this way, we kept disappearing all through Andalusia, a country of yellow earth and yellow sky, to my eyes an immense chamberpot flooded with sunlight, where each day, as a new character, I raped a likewise transformed Simone, especially towards noon, on the ground and in the blazing sun, under the reddish eyes of Sir Edmond.

On the fourth day, at Gibraltar, the Englishman purchased a yacht, and we set sail towards new adventures with a crew of Negroes.

Part Two

COINCIDENCES

While composing this partly imaginary tale, I was struck by several coincidences, and since they appeared indirectly to bring out the meaning of what I have written, I would like to describe them.

I began writing with no precise goal, animated chiefly by a desire to forget, at least for the time being, the things I can be or do personally. Thus, at first, I thought that the character speaking in the first person had no relation to me. But then one day I was looking through an American magazine filled with photographs of European landscapes, and I chanced upon two astonishing pictures: the first was a street in the practically unknown village from which my family comes; the second, the nearby ruins of a medieval fortified castle on a crag in the mountain. I promptly recalled an episode in my life, connected to those ruins. At the time, I was twenty-one; vacationing in the village that summer, I decided one evening to go to the ruins that same night, and did so immediately, accompanied by several perfectly chaste girls and, as a chaperone, my mother. I was in love with one of the girls, and she shared my feelings, yet we had never spoken to one another because she believed she had a religious calling, which she wanted to examine in all liberty. After walking for some one and half hours, we arrived at the foot of the castle around ten or eleven in a rather gloomy night. We had started climbing the rocky mountain with its utterly romantic wall, when a white and thoroughly luminous ghost leapt forth from a deep cavity in the rocks and barred our way. It was so extraordinary that one girl and my mother fell back together, and the others let out piercing shrieks. I myself felt a sudden terror, which stifled my voice, and so it took me a few seconds before I could hurl some threats, which were unintelligible to the phantom, even though I was certain from the very beginning that it was all a hoax. The phantom did flee the moment he saw me striding towards him, and I didn't let him out of my sight until I recognized my older brother, who had biked up with another boy. Wearing a sheet, he had succeeded in scaring us by popping out under the sudden ray of an acetylene lantern.

The day I found the photograph in the magazine, I had just finished the sheet episode in the story, and I noticed that I kept seeing the sheet at the left, just as the sheeted ghost had appeared at the left, and I realized there was a perfect coincidence of images tied to analogous upheavals. Indeed, I have rarely been as dumbfounded as at the apparition of the false phantom.

I was very astonished at having unknowingly substituted a perfectly obscene image for a vision apparently devoid of any sexual implication. Still, I would soon have cause for even greater astonishment.

I had already thought out all the details of the scene in the Seville vestry, especially the incision in the priest's socket and the plucking of his eye, when, realizing the kinship between the story and my own life, I amused myself by introducing the description of a tragic bullfight that I had actually witnessed. Oddly enough, I drew no connection between the two episodes until I did a precise description of the injury inflicted on Manuel Granero (a real person) by the bull; but the moment I reached this death scene, I was totally taken aback. The opening of the priest's eye was not, as I had believed, a gratuitous invention. I was merely transfering, to a different person, an image that had most likely led a very profound life. If I devised the business about snipping out the priest's eye, it was because I had seen a bull's horn tear out a matador's eye. Thus, precisely the two images that probably most upset me had sprung from the darkest corner of my memory—and in a scarcely recognizable shape—as soon as I gave myself over to lewd dreams.

But no sooner did I realize this (I had just

finished portraying the bullfight of May 7) than I visited a friend of mine, who is a doctor. I read the description to him, but it was not in the same form as now. Never having seen the skinned balls of a bull, I assumed they were the same bright red color as the erect cock of the animal, and that was how they were depicted in the first draft. The entire *Story of the Eye* was woven in my mind out of two ancient and closely associated obsessions, *eggs* and *eyes,* but nevertheless, I had previously regarded the balls of the bull as independent of that cycle. Yet when I finished reading to him, my friend remarked that I had absolutely no idea of what the glands I was writing about were really like, and he promptly read aloud a detailed description in an anatomical textbook. I thus learned that human or animal balls are egg-shaped and look the same as an eyeball.

This time, I ventured to explain such extraordinary relations by assuming a profound region of my mind, where certain images coincide, the elementary ones, the *completely obscene* ones, i.e., the most scandalous, precisely those on which the conscious floats indefinitely, unable to endure them without an explosion or aberration.

However, upon locating this breaking point of the conscious or, if you will, the favorite place of sexual deviation, certain quite different personal memories were quickly associated with some harrowing images that had emerged during an obscene composition.

When I was born, my father was suffering from general paralysis, and he was already blind when he conceived me; not long after my birth, his sinister disease confined him to an armchair. However, the very contrary of most male babies, who are in love with their mothers, I was in love with my father. Now the following was connected to his paralysis and blindness. He was unable to go and urinate in the toilet like most people; instead, he did it into a small container at his armchair, and since he had to urinate very often, he was unembarrassed about doing it in front of me, under a blanket, which, since he was blind, he usually placed askew. But the weirdest thing was certainly the way he looked while pissing. Since he could not see anything, his pupils very frequently pointed up into space, shifting under the lids, and this happened particularly when he pissed. Furthermore, he had huge, ever-gaping eyes that flanked an eagle nose, and those huge eyes went almost entirely blank when he pissed, with a completely stupefying expression of abandon and aberration in a world that he alone could see and that aroused his vaguely sardonic and absent laugh (I would have liked to recall everything here at once, for instance the erratic nature of a blind man's isolated laughter, and so forth). In any case, the image of those white *eyes* from that time was directly linked, for me, to the image of eggs, and that explains the almost regular appearance of urine every time *eyes* or *eggs* occur in the story.

After perceiving this kinship between distinct elements, I was led to discover a further, no less essential kinship between the general nature of my story and a particular fact.

I was about fourteen when my affection for my father turned into a deep and unconscious hatred. I began vaguely enjoying his constant shrieks at the lightning pains caused by the tabes, which are considered among the worst pains known to man. Furthermore, the filthy, smelly state to which his total disablement often reduced him (for instance, he sometimes left shit on his pants) was not nearly so disagreeable to me as I thought. Then again, in all things, I adopted the attitudes and opinions most radically opposed to those of that supremely nauseating creature.

One night, we were awakened, my mother and I, by vehement words that the syphilitic was literally howling in his room: he had suddenly gone mad. I went for the doctor, who came immediately. My father kept endlessly and eloquently imagining the most outrageous and generally the happiest events. The doctor had withdrawn to the next room with my mother and I had remained with the blind lunatic, when he shrieked in a stentorian voice: "Doctor, let me know when you're done fucking my wife!" For me, that utterance, which in a split second annihilated the demoralizing effects of a strict upbringing, left me with something like a steady obligation, unconscious and unwilled: the necessity of finding an equivalent to that sentence in any situation I happen to be in; and this largely explains *Story of the Eye.* To complete this survey of the high summits of my personal obscenity, I must add a final connection I made in regard to Marcelle. It was one of the most disconcerting, and I did not arrive at it until the very end.

It is impossible for me to say positively that Marcelle is basically identical with my mother. Such a statement would actually be, if not false, then at least exaggerated. Thus Marcelle is also a fourteen-year-old girl who once sat opposite me for a quarter of an hour at the Café des deux Magots in Paris. Nonetheless, I still want to tell about some memories that ultimately fastened a few episodes to unmistakable facts.

Soon after my father's attack of lunacy, my mother, *at the end of a vile scene to which her mother subjected her in front of me, suddenly lost her mind too.* She spent several months in a crisis of manic-depressive insanity (melancholy). The absurd ideas of damnation and catastrophe that seized control of her irritated me even more because I was forced to look after her continually. She was in such a bad state that one night I removed some candlesticks with marble bases from my room; I was afraid she might kill me while I slept. On the other hand, whenever I lost patience, I went so far as to strike her, violently twisting her wrists to try and bring her to her senses.

One day, my mother disappeared while our backs were turned; we hunted her for a long time and finally found her *hanged* in the attic. However, they managed to revive her.

A short time later, she disappeared again, this time at night; I myself went looking for her, endlessly, along a creek, wherever she might have tried to drown herself. Running without stopping, through the darkness, across swamps, I at last found myself face to face with her: *she was drenched up to her belt, the skirt was pissing the creek water,* but she had come out on her own, and the icy, wintery water was not very deep anyway.

I never linger over such memories, for they have long since lost any emotional significance for me. There was no way I could restore them to life except by transforming them and making them unrecognizable, at first glance, to my eyes, solely because during that deformation they acquired the lewdest of meanings.

 W.C.

A year before *Story of the Eye,* I had written a book entitled *W.C.*: a small book, a rather crazy piece of writing. *W.C.* was as lugubrious as *Story of the Eye* was juvenile. The manuscript of *W.C.* was burnt but that was no loss, considering my present sadness: it was a shriek of horror (horror at myself, not for my debauchery, but for the philosopher's head in which since then . . . how sad it is!). On the other hand, I am as happy as ever with the fulminating joy of *The Eye*: nothing can wipe it away. Such joy, bordering on naive folly, will forever remain beyond terror, for terror reveals its meaning.

A drawing for *W.C.* showed an eye: the scaffold's eye. Solitary, solar, bristling with lashes, it gazed from the lunette of a guillotine. The drawing was named *The Eternal Return,* and its horrible machine was the crossbeam, gymnastic gallows, portico. Coming from the horizon, the road to eternity passed through it. A parodistic verse, heard in a sketch at the *Concert Mayol,* supplied the caption:

> *God, how the corpse's blood is sad*
> *in the depth of sound.*

Story of the Eye has another reminiscence of *W.C.,* which appears on the title page, placing all that follows under the worst of signs. The name Lord Auch [pronounced ōsh] refers to a habit of a friend of mine; when vexed, instead of saying "aux chiottes!" [to the shithouse], he would shorten it to "aux ch'." *Lord* is English for God (in the Scriptures): Lord Auch is God relieving himself. The story is too lively to dwell upon; every creature transfigured by such a place: God sinking into it rejuvenates the heavens.

To be God, naked, solar, in the rainy night, on a field: red, divinely, manuring with the majesty of a tempest, the face grimacing, torn apart, being IMPOSSIBLE in tears: who knew, before me, what majesty is?

The "eye of the conscience" and the "woods of justice" incarnate the eternal return, and is there any more desperate image for remorse?

I gave the author of *W.C.* the pseudonym of Troppmann.

I jerked off naked, at night, by my mother's corpse. (A few people, reading *Coincidences*, wondered whether it did not have the fictional character of the tale itself. But, like this *Preface*, *Coincidences* has a literal exactness: many people in the village of R. could confirm the material; moreover, some of my friends did read *W.C.*)

What upset me more was: seeing my father shit a great number of times. He would get out of his blind paralytic's bed (my father being both blind and paralytic at once). It was very hard for him to get out of bed (I would help him) and settle on a chamber-pot, in his nightshirt and, usually, a cotton nightcap (he had a pointed gray beard, ill-kempt, a large eagle-nose, and immense hollow eyes staring into space). At times, the "lightning-sharp pains" would make him howl like a beast, sticking out his bent leg, which he futilely hugged in his arms.

My father having conceived me when blind

(absolutely blind), I cannot tear out my eyes like Oedipus.

Like Oedipus, I solved the riddle: no one divined it more deeply than I.

On November 6, 1915, in a bombarded town, a few miles from the German lines, my father died in abandonment.

My mother and I had abandoned him during the German advance in August 1914.

We left him with the housekeeper.

The Germans occupied the town, then evacuated it. We could now return: my mother, unable to bear the thought of it, went mad. Late that year, my mother recovered: she refused to let me go home to N. We received occasional letters from my father, he just barely ranted and raved. When we learned he was dying, my mother agreed to go with me. He died a few days before our arrival, asking for his children: we found a sealed coffin in the bedroom.

When my father went mad (a year before the war) after a hallucinating night, my mother sent me to the post office to dispatch a telegram. I remember being struck with a horrible pride en route. Misery overwhelmed me, internal irony replied: "So much horror makes you predestined": a few months earlier, one fine morning in December, I had informed my parents, who were beside themselves, that I would never set foot in high school again. No amount of anger could change my mind:

I lived alone, going out seldom, by way of the fields, avoiding the center, where I might have run into friends.

My father, an unreligious man, died refusing to see the priest. During puberty, I was unreligious myself (my mother indifferent). But I went to a priest in August 1914; and until 1920, rarely did I let a week go by without confessing my sins! In 1920, I changed again, I stopped believing in anything but my future chances. My piety was merely an attempt at evasion: I wanted to escape my destiny at any price, I was abandoning my father. Today, I know I am "blind," immeasurable, I am man "abandoned" on the globe like my father at N. No one on earth or in heaven cared about my father's dying terror. Still, I believe he faced up to it, as always. What a "horrible pride," at moments, in Dad's blind smile!

[Preface to *Story of the Eye*
from *Le Petit*: 1943]

Outline of a Sequel to Story of the Eye

After fifteen years of more and more serious debauchery, Simone ends up in a torture camp. But by mistake; descriptions of torture, tears, imbecility of unhappiness, Simone at the threshold of a conversion, exhorted by a cadaverous woman, one more in the series of devotees of the Church of Seville. She is now thirty-five. Beautiful when entering the camp, but old age is gradually taking over, irremediable. Beautiful scene with a female torturer and the devotee; the devotee and Simone are beaten to death, Simone escapes temptation.

She dies as though making love, but in the purity (chaste) and the *imbecility* of death: fever and agony transfigure her. The torturer strikes her, she is indifferent to the blows, indifferent to the words of the devotee, lost in the labor of agony. It is by no means an erotic joy, it is far more than that. But with no result. Nor is it masochistic, and, profoundly, this exaltation is beyond any imagining; it surpasses everything. However, its basis is solitude and absence.

(from the fourth edition, 1967)